There's No Business Like Show Business

Nancy, Bess, and George clapped as Carla strutted onstage in a colorful Spanish flamenco costume. Her hands clacked a pair of castanets. But when she kicked up her heels, they didn't get very far—thick wads of green chewing gum were stuck to the soles of her shoes!

Carla looked horrified as her shoes began sticking to the stage. She finally stopped dancing, tears in her eyes.

"Someone must have stuck the gum on my shoes!" Carla cried.

NANCY DREW

#30 AND THE CLUE CREW®

Dance Off

By CAROLYN KEENE

ILLUSTRATED BY MACKY PAMINTUAN

SCHOLASTIC INC.

ISBN 978-0-545-56860-9

Text copyright © 2011 by Simon & Schuster, Inc. Illustrations copyright © 2011 by Macky Pamintuan. All rights reserved. Published by Scholastic Inc., 557 Broadway, New York, NY 10012, by arrangement with Aladdin Paperbacks, an imprint of Simon & Schuster Children's Publishing Division. NANCY DREW and NANCY DREW AND THE CLUE CREW are registered trademarks of Simon & Schuster, Inc. SCHOLASTIC and associated logos are trademarks and/or registered trademarks of Scholastic Inc.

12 11 10 9 8 7   16 17 18/0

Printed in the U.S.A.   40

First Scholastic printing, April 2013

Designed by Lisa Vega
The text of this book was set in ITC Stone Informal.

CONTENTS

CHAPTER ONE

Fans and Cancans

"Why do we have to wear these goofy pink coats?" George Fayne asked. She frowned at the vinyl coat draped over her arm. "What detectives walk around in these?"

"Dancing detectives!" Nancy Drew replied.

"Just like us!" Bess Marvin added happily.

The Clue Crew never wore pink trench coats when they worked on their cases. But the coats and giant magnifying glasses were the perfect costume for their big dance number.

"Who cares if they look funny or squeak when we move?" Nancy asked her two best friends. "We're about to audition for *Kids Can Dance!*—one of the hottest shows on TV!"

1

"And meet Bryce Brown!" Bess squealed.

Nancy squealed along with Bess. Fourteen-year-old Bryce Brown was the singing, dancing star of the girls' other favorite show, *Middle School Meltdown*. He was also one of the judges for the auditions.

"Don't forget," Nancy said excitedly, "the winning prize is a chance to dance on *Middle School Meltdown*."

"And a one-thousand-dollar check," Bess added. She turned to George. "What would you do with the prize money?"

"Buy a new coat," George groaned.

Bess heaved a sigh. She and George were cousins but different in every way. Bess had blond hair, blue eyes, and fashion-forward clothes. George had dark hair and eyes and the coolest computer gadgets and gizmos. George didn't mind being called a computer geek as long as she wasn't called Georgia—her real name!

Nancy, Bess, and George hurried down River Street toward the River Heights Spotlight Theater.

That's where the auditions would be held for the next few days.

It was only Thursday, and the girls weren't auditioning until Sunday. But everyone had to bring their costumes and music to the theater that afternoon.

"Remember, Clue Crew, no mysteries until the auditions are over," Nancy said. "We have to—"

"Nancy!" Bess cut in as she looked back over her shoulder. "We're being chased by a giant ice-cream cone!"

"Huh?" Nancy turned around and gasped.

Sure enough, a giant ice-cream cone with arms and legs was racing toward them yelling, "Wait up! Wait up!"

George rolled her eyes and said, "That's not ice cream. That's just Henderson."

The cone came closer. Nancy could see Henderson "Drippy" Murphy's face underneath the plastic swirl head.

Henderson's dad drove the Mr. Drippy ice-cream truck. But that did not explain the ice-cream costume.

"Where are you going looking like that?" Nancy asked.

"Same place you are!" Henderson answered. "I'm trying out for *Kids Can Dance!*"

Henderson's shoes tapped on the sidewalk as

he danced for the girls. He then lifted his foot to show the steel tap on the bottom of his shoe.

"It's my dad's idea," Henderson sighed. "He needs the prize money so he can buy a pretzel truck for the winter."

"Because it's too cold to sell ice cream?" Nancy asked.

Henderson nodded and said, "My dad needs a job badly."

"Good luck, then!" Bess said before George jabbed her with her elbow. "I mean, good luck—but I hope we still win."

The brown brick theater with the marquee was only a few steps away. Practicing their dance numbers outside were many kids Nancy knew from school. Some wore their costumes over their street clothes just like Henderson did.

The fourth-grade Gleason twins danced the minuet dressed in old-fashioned clothes and towering white wigs.

A group of fifth-grade girls wore cheerleader uniforms as they shook colorful pom-poms and practiced their splits. A few feet away Kendra Jackson, from the girls' third-grade class, kicked her leg under a long, ruffled skirt.

"She's a French cancan dancer," Bess whispered.

"Speaking of cans, check that out," George said.

The girls turned to watch Antonio Elefano and Peter Patino dancing stiffly in robot costumes made from jumbo tin cans. Hip-hop music blared from their silver boom box.

"Better quit now, Clue Crew!" Antonio shouted. "Because the Rip-It-Up Robots are going to take the prize!"

"You already take the cake!" George shouted back.

Nancy pulled George away from the boys. She refused to let the two biggest pests at school spoil an awesome day.

"I wish my dad could watch us audition," Nancy said, flipping her reddish blond bangs aside. "I wonder why parents aren't allowed."

"Because the show is afraid they'd be too

pushy," George explained. "Like some stage moms and dads can be."

"Like her," Bess whispered. She pointed at a tall, blond woman wearing a white pantsuit. "That's Cookie, Bryce's mom-ager."

"Mom-ager?" Nancy repeated.

"Part mom, part manager," Bess explained.

"And full-time screamer," George muttered.

Cookie was arguing loudly with another woman standing near the theater door.

"Bryce has just landed a part in a huge movie!" Cookie was shouting. "He must fly to Hollywood—ASAP!"

"He has a contract," the other woman said.

"Mindy, you're the producer of *Kids Can Dance!*," Cookie huffed. "Release him from his contract this instant!"

"Sorry, Cookie," Mindy said, shaking her head.

Cookie's eyes narrowed as she said, "Oh, you'll be sorry, all right!"

Whoa, Nancy thought. *I hope Bryce is a lot nicer than his mom.*

Mindy turned away from Cookie to open the theater door. She first made the kids line up, then led them into the theater. They were directed backstage, where they hung up their costumes. George stood on tiptoes as she put their dance music CD on a shelf with the others.

"Do you think somebody will steal our pink coats?" Bess asked as they left the back room.

"If we're lucky," George joked.

The girls found three seats next to one another and sat down. From there they could see the judges' table set in front of the stage. But where were the judges?

"Hi, kids!" Mayor Strong called out as he walked out on the stage. "Who's ready to kick it up?"

Cheers filled the theater. Nancy shivered with excitement. This was it!

"First let's meet the judges," Mayor Strong said, turning toward the wings. "Straight from Hollywood, please welcome choreographer to the stars—Ivy Hedges!"

A smiling Ivy waved as she ran onto the stage. She walked down to the judges' table, still waving.

"Next—all the way from London, England, former ballet star Nigel Pemberton!" Mayor Strong announced.

Nigel hardly looked at the kids as he joined Ivy at the table. He wasn't smiling, either.

"Last but not least," Mayor Strong announced, "you know him from *Middle School Meltdown*— Bryce Brown!"

"Aaaaa!"

"Eeeee!"

"Omigosh!!!"

Nancy squeezed Bess's hand as they shrieked too. Running onto the stage was the star himself—Bryce Brown!

"He's cuter in person than he is on TV!" Bess squealed, practically digging her nails into George's arm.

"Ouch!" George complained.

Bryce was wearing a *Middle School Meltdown*

jacket and faded jeans. "Who's ready to burn the floor?" he shouted.

A louder scream answered Bryce's question. But nobody was screaming louder than Ivy!

"I didn't know Ivy liked Bryce too," Nancy said.

"I don't think she's screaming for Bryce," George said, staring straight at the judges' table.

"Then why is she screaming?" Bess asked.

George gulped and then said, "Because there's something big, gray, and furry under that table!"

ChAPTER TWO

Stage Fright

Nancy's jaw dropped as Bryce and Nigel lifted the table. Crouched underneath was a giant squirrel!

But as the squirrel stood up Nancy saw it was not a squirrel at all.

"You guys!" Nancy exclaimed. "It's Phoebe Frankel from the second grade."

Mindy seemed to recognize Phoebe too.

"Didn't you sign up to audition yesterday?" Mindy asked Phoebe. "And didn't we say you had to be eight to ten years old to audition?"

"Yes," Phoebe said, nodding her furry head. "But I'm going to be eight years old in a few months."

The audience snickered.

"And," Phoebe went on, "my grandfather owns this theater, so I thought it would be okay."

Before Mindy could stop her, Phoebe jumped up on the stage. Her bushy tail bobbed as she swayed back and forth.

"I call my dance a salute to fall!" Phoebe said as she twirled around the stage. "Squirrels collect nuts in the fall, you know."

"Can somebody collect that nut and get her out of here?" Nigel barked.

A gray-haired man angrily marched up to Nigel and said, "Watch how you talk to my granddaughter, buddy!"

"That must be Lou

Frankel," George whispered. "He owns the Spotlight Theater."

"Oh," Nancy whispered back. George never went anywhere without researching it on the computer first.

"Gentlemen, gentlemen!" Mayor Strong said, pushing his way between Lou and Nigel. "If Phoebe can't dance, perhaps she can have a little job instead."

"What kind of job?" Phoebe asked, jumping up and down. "Can I be Bryce's personal assistant? Can I? Can I?"

Nancy saw Bryce shake his head at Mindy, ever so slightly.

"I have an idea," Mindy blurted. "Why doesn't Phoebe help the dancers as they get ready to audition?"

"You mean the other kids?" Phoebe cried.

"Go for it, cupcake," Lou told Phoebe. "One day this theater will be yours. Might as well learn something!"

Phoebe's squirrel tail drooped sadly. Nancy could see how badly she wanted to audition for *Kids Can Dance!*

"Whatever," Phoebe said, and sighed.

"Good!" Mindy said with a grin. "Why don't you go backstage and help the first kids about to audition?"

"Yeah, squirrelly!" Antonio yelled from the audience. "Get them some lemonade."

"And hold the acorns!" Peter guffawed.

Phoebe ignored the boys as she sulked on her way backstage.

"Well, now," Mayor Strong said cheerily. "I guess there's no business like show business."

After the judges were settled at their table, Mindy introduced the first act. "Please give a shout-out for fifth-grader Carla Mendoza!"

Nancy, Bess, and George clapped as Carla strutted onstage in a colorful Spanish flamenco costume. Her hands clacked a pair of castanets. But when she kicked up her heels, they didn't get very far—thick wads of green chewing gum were stuck to the soles of her shoes!

"Yuck!" Bess cried.

Carla looked horrified as her shoes began sticking to the stage. She finally stopped dancing, tears in her eyes.

"It's okay, Carla," Ivy said sweetly. "Everyone steps in gum at least once in their life."

"But I didn't see any gum on the floor!" Carla cried. "Someone must have stuck them on my shoes."

"A likely excuse," Nigel said, and sighed loudly. "We should change the name of this show to *Kids Can Dance* Except *in River Heights!*"

Nancy gulped. She hoped Nigel wouldn't be as mean when they auditioned on Sunday.

The rest of the auditions went smoothly. But Nancy couldn't stop thinking about Carla's sticky, icky shoes. Did someone stick gum on her shoes like she said?

"More auditions tomorrow," Mayor Strong announced when the auditions were over. "See you after school!"

The kids filed out of the theater. Nancy smiled when she saw Hannah Gruen waiting outside.

Hannah had been the Drews' housekeeper since Nancy was only three years old. She couldn't replace Nancy's mother, who died. But with her hugs, cookies, and reminders to wear sweaters and brush her teeth, she came pretty close.

"Thanks for picking us up, Hannah," Nancy said.

"No problem," Hannah said. "But don't you girls want to get an autograph from your fave before you go home?"

Nancy looked to see where Hannah was pointing. Cookie was outside the theater handing out pictures of Bryce.

"Totally!" Nancy gasped excitedly. She and her friends ran to get autographed pictures.

But when Bess looked at her picture, she shook her head and said, "This isn't Bryce's handwriting. And I know everything about Bryce Brown."

Nancy believed Bess. Her friend read every magazine with an article on Bryce. She even visited his website every day.

"If Bryce didn't sign it, who did?" Nancy asked.

The girls turned to Cookie. One kid was complaining that her picture had no autograph. Cookie grabbed the picture, pulled out a pen, and signed Bryce's name herself!

"That's who!" George muttered.

Nancy frowned, then whispered, "For a Cookie she's not very sweet."

Besides Saturday and Sunday, Friday was Nancy's favorite day. But this Friday was extra special. Right after school Mrs. Fayne picked the girls up and drove them to the Spotlight Theater for the second day of auditions.

As Nancy, Bess, and George filed into the theater to watch the others try out, they saw Phoebe. Her hair was sticking out in all directions, and her arms were filled with plastic water bottles!

"Help me find my ballet shoes!" Deirdre Shannon shouted from the backstage door. "I don't see them anywhere."

"What took you so long with that water?" Antonio demanded. "My mouth is so dry I'm spitting cotton balls!"

"Okay!" Phoebe shouted back. She gave the girls a quick glance. "I hate this job, and I hate *Kids Can Dance!*"

"I guess you can't blame her," Bess whispered as Phoebe ran backstage.

The girls were happy to find three seats next to one another in the first row this time.

"We're right behind the judges' table!" Bess squeaked.

"In two days we'll be up on that stage auditioning too," Nancy said dreamily.

"That's why we have to practice all day tomorrow," Bess said firmly. "So we don't make fools of ourselves like that poor flamenco dancer."

"We're already making fools of ourselves," George mumbled. "In those pink coats."

"Shh! Here come the judges," Nancy pointed out.

Ivy, Nigel, and Bryce took their seats behind the judges' table.

"We're so close to Bryce." Bess swooned. "I can see how brown his eyes are!"

"I can see how his hair curls just a bit at the ends!" Nancy sighed.

"I can see a zit on his cheek," George murmured.

After welcoming the audience, Mayor Strong introduced the first act.

"Please welcome Deirdre Shannon," Mayor Strong said, "dancing the part of the dying swan from *Swan Lake*."

A boy in the audience yawned loudly. Soon the theater was filled with the sound of soft classical music. Deirdre flitted out from the wings on her tiptoes, gracefully flapping her arms up and down. But the minute she began to dance . . .

Tap, tap, tap, tap, tap . . .

"Omigosh," Bess whispered. "It sounds like she has taps on her ballet shoes."

Deirdre's face turned tomato red when she realized what was happening.

"Stop the music this instant," Nigel commanded. "That was not a swan—it was a turkey."

"But it's not my fault!" Deirdre cried. "Someone glued taps on my ballet slippers!"

"Sure they did, dear," Ivy said gently.

Deirdre was still protesting as Mindy whisked her offstage.

"All righty then," Mayor Strong told

the audience. "Let's give it up for our next dancers—the fifth-grade Cheer Brigade!"

Peppy music blared as six cheerleaders ran onto the stage, smiling brightly. As they danced Nancy noticed clouds of white dust billowing from their pom-poms! One by one the girls stopped dancing to scratch their necks, their arms, and even their legs!

"Sorry!" a tall cheerleader with red hair said. She held up one pom-pom. "It's like someone put itching powder in our pom-poms."

Nancy's eyes widened. Itching powder?

"And I'm itching to get on to the next act," Nigel huffed. "What's wrong with River Heights, anyway?"

The cheerleaders were still itching and scratching as they hurried off into the wings.

"I apologize to the judges," Mayor Strong declared. "I don't know why our dancers are messing up!"

Nancy did the math: One fallen flamenco dancer, one tapped-out ballerina, and six chafing cheerleaders equaled something fishy.

"The dancers of River Heights aren't messing up," Nancy whispered to her friends. "Someone is messing up the dancers."

CHAPTER THREE

Gag Order

"You mean someone is doing this on purpose?" Bess asked, her blue eyes flashing.

"Or maybe it's just a fluke," George said. "I'll bet nothing happens to the next act."

"I *hope* nothing happens," Nancy added.

The next act was the Gleason twins, dressed in eighteenth-century costume and dancing the minuet. The audience laughed as what looked like rubber cockroaches spilled out of Gina's and Gilbert's tall white wigs!

"As our glorious Queen Victoria once said," Nigel declared, "'I am *not amused.'*"

"N-n-neither am I, Mr. Pemberton," Mayor Strong stammered. "That I can assure you."

"Now do you believe me?" Nancy whispered.

Bess and George both nodded.

"Kids!" Mindy announced. "If you can't stop clowning around, we'll have to cancel the River Heights auditions."

"No!" the kids in the audience cried.

"Yes!" a voice cheered. "Yes! Yes! Yes!"

Nancy turned to see Cookie. She was standing at the side of the theater grinning smugly.

"We've got to find out who's doing this," Nancy said. "To save River Heights from looking bad."

"And us from looking bad," Bess pointed out. "We're auditioning in two days, remember?"

"I thought we weren't going to be detectives this week," George said. "Only dancers."

"There *won't* be any dancing if we don't solve this case," Nancy said. She and her friends stood up and slipped out of the theater.

"Let's go to our headquarters," Nancy said, buttoning up her bulky sweater. "And get to work."

Nancy, Bess, and George all had to follow the same rule: They could walk up to five blocks together as long as it was still light outside and they were together.

After crunching through five blocks of fallen leaves, the girls reached the Drew house. Once inside, they went straight upstairs to Nancy's room.

"Get away from the computer, Bess," George complained. "That's my job!"

"It's Nancy's computer!" Bess insisted. "And she said I could check out Bryce's website first."

"Quickly," Nancy reminded.

"Wow!" Bess said with her eyes glued to the screen. "There's a whole page about Bryce's visit to River Heights. He and Cookie are staying at the Glitz-Morton Hotel!"

"Enough information," George said. She waved Bess away from the computer and sat down. After opening a new file for their case, the Clue Crew got to work.

"Where do you think the rubber cockroaches and the itching powder came from?" Bess asked.

"Yuks Joke Shop, where else?" Nancy said. "I'll bet the gum did too. I never saw gum as sticky as that!"

"Those taps on Deirdre's ballet slippers had to come from tap shoes," George said as she typed.

"But who would want to mess up the dance auditions?" Bess wondered out loud.

"Probably someone who was mad at the dancers or the show," George decided.

The word "mad" made Nancy think of Phoebe.

"Phoebe Frankel was mad that she didn't get to audition," Nancy pointed out. "She was mad at the kids for bossing her around too."

"Phoebe was backstage with the dancers," Bess added. "And her grandfather owns the theater, so she'd have plenty of chances to sneak back there even after everybody left."

"Don't forget to put Antonio and Peter on our suspect list," Bess said.

"What reason would the boys have for ruining the auditions?" Nancy asked.

"They're pests," Bess replied. "What better reason is that?"

Nancy plopped down on the edge of her bed. She knew there was another suspect, but as hard as she tried she couldn't think of his or her name.

"Cookie break!" Hannah said, carrying a plate of oatmeal cookies into the room. As she left the room Nancy's eyes lit up.

"Cookie!" Nancy exclaimed, jumping from the bed. "Bryce's mom-ager was arguing with Mindy about getting Bryce out of the show!"

"Cookie also said Mindy would be sorry," Bess said. "Whatever that meant."

"We've got to find Cookie and ask her some questions," Nancy said, narrowing her eyes.

Bess grabbed an oatmeal cookie. Before taking a bite, she said, "How are we going to question Cookie Brown?"

Nancy gulped as she remembered Cookie yelling at Mindy. "Carefully," she replied. "Very, very carefully!"

"One of the rubber cockroaches fell into Nigel's lap, Daddy!" Nancy said later that evening. "It wasn't funny, but it was kind of funny. Do you know what I mean?"

Mr. Drew nodded. He and Nancy had just finished dinner. They were now in the den deciding what to watch on TV.

"I wish I could have been there," Mr. Drew

said. "But you know what they said—"

"No parents allowed," Nancy finished. "Unless you're somebody's mom-ager."

Nancy's puppy, Chocolate Chip, padded into the den. She nuzzled her nose in Nancy's palm.

Mr. Drew picked up the remote and clicked on the TV. A commercial was on for a juice called Fruity Fizzy. Nancy grinned when she saw who was singing the jingle.

"Bryce!" Nancy squealed.

Chip barked, startled by Nancy's voice.

"Rock me, Fruity Fizzy!" Bryce sang as he danced. "Tastes so good it makes me dizzy!"

"He's . . . so . . . cool." Nancy swooned at the TV.

"I thought I was your favorite guy, Nancy," Mr. Drew said, pretending to look hurt.

Nancy smiled at her dad. He wasn't just the best lawyer in River Heights—he was the best dad in the world!

"You'll always be my favorite, Daddy," Nancy insisted. "Besides, Bryce and I have absolutely nothing in common."

"Really?" Mr. Drew asked. "How come?"

"Fruity Fizzy makes my nose tickle," Nancy giggled.

Nancy and her dad decided to watch a show about polar bears. But as much as Nancy loved polar bears, she couldn't pay attention to the TV.

I can't wait to go to the auditions tomorrow to work on our new case, Nancy thought as she relaxed on the sofa next to Chip. *Of course—seeing Bryce again will be pretty cool too.*

❀ ❀ ❀

"You want to go to Yuks?" George asked the next morning. "What about the auditions?"

Nancy watched a gold leaf drop on her shoulder as she walked with Bess and George. It was Saturday morning, and the girls had permission to walk together to River Street.

"There's plenty of time before the auditions start," Nancy said. "I want to ask some questions—like who bought the rubber bugs and itching powder."

"I still think Antonio and Peter messed up the auditions," Bess said. "Remember when they snuck that whoopee cushion on our substitute teacher's chair? Where do you think they bought that?"

Yuks Joke Shop was just down the block. Nancy could see the door swing open. A boy was stepping out. But it was not Antonio or Peter.

"It's Henderson," Nancy said.

Henderson had a big grin on his face—like

he knew something nobody else did. He didn't seem to see the girls as he turned and walked the other way.

"Wait a minute," George said slowly. "Didn't Henderson say his dad needed the prize money for a pretzel truck?"

"And didn't Henderson have taps on his shoes?" Nancy added. "And didn't he just come out of Yuks?"

"Yes . . . yes . . . and yes!" Bess said, answering each question.

"Then I think we have one more suspect," Nancy said very slowly. "Henderson 'Drippy' Murphy."

CHAPTER FOUR

Fave Rave

Henderson had turned the corner and was out of sight.

"Let's go inside Yuks," Nancy suggested. "We can ask if Henderson bought anything in the last three days."

"And *what* he bought!" Bess added.

The girls filed into the joke store. Nancy's mouth dropped open when she saw Mr. Decker behind the counter. The owner had an arrow straight through his head!

"It's not real—it's another gag," George whispered.

The girls' eyes darted around the store. Masks dangled from the ceiling—funny and creepy.

There were racks of costumes and piles of boxes marked: FAKE EYEBALLS, GARLIC GUM, HAND BUZZERS, PLASTIC FANGS—and more.

"Early Halloween shopping?" Mr. Decker asked.

"Not yet," Nancy said. "We just want to know if Henderson Murphy bought anything in this store."

Mr. Decker pointed to a sign behind the counter. It read: ALL SALES CONFIDENTIAL.

"See that?" Mr. Decker asked. "That means

that all sales here are completely top secret."

"Top secret?" George said, wrinkling her nose.

"That's right," Mr. Decker said. "If you buy witchy warts or a squirting toilet seat—your secret is safe with me."

"But a crime was committed," Nancy protested.

"Ahhh! Stop it, girls," Mr. Decker said, pointing to the arrow. "Can't you see you're giving me a headache?"

Nancy looked past Mr. Decker at a glossy photo taped to the wall. It was an autographed picture of Bryce.

"Was Bryce Brown here too?" Nancy asked.

"Confidential!" Mr. Decker shouted.

The girls turned and ran out of the store.

"A big help he was!" George snorted.

"How do you think that picture of Bryce got there?" Nancy wondered out loud.

"Cookie gives out Bryce's autographs," Bess said.

Cookie? A slow smile spread across Nancy's face.

"So Cookie was shopping at Yuks Joke Shop," Nancy said. "I guess not *everything* in that store is top secret."

Nancy's thoughts were interrupted by a bunch of screams. She turned to see a crowd of girls standing in front of a hotel down the block: the Glitz-Morton.

"That's the hotel Bryce is staying in," Bess said.

Nancy, Bess, and George walked over to the fanciest hotel in River Heights. A crowd was waving Bryce's picture in the air and shouting Bryce's name.

"I want to get inside that hotel," Nancy whispered.

"So do all those other girls," George pointed out.

"I don't want to find Bryce," Nancy said. "I want to find Cookie so we can ask her some questions."

"Good luck." Bess pointed to a policeman standing before the barricade. "Police Chief McGinnis is making sure nobody gets in."

"You're right," Nancy sighed.

The girls watched as a doorman began unloading a guest's car. He hooked several long black garment bags on the bar of a rolling luggage rack.

"If we can't check in," George whispered, "why don't we *sneak* in?"

The doorman turned his back to the cart. Quickly, George hopped onto the luggage rack, slipping between two garment bags. Her hand jutted out to wave her friends aboard.

Nancy and Bess followed, slipping between the hanging bags. Nancy held her breath as she heard the doorman say, "I'll wheel your luggage into the lobby while the valet parks your car."

The cart began to roll. Nancy's teeth rattled as it jumped over a crack in the sidewalk. When the cart came to a stop, the girls slowly peeked out. They were in a huge room decorated with velvet sofas and towering green plants. A marble floor glistened like an ice-skating rink.

"It's the hotel lobby," Nancy hissed.

The girls waited till the coast was clear. While the doorman pressed the elevator button, they jumped off the luggage cart. They crouched and hid behind one of the potted plants.

"Wow!" Bess whispered. "This hotel is like a palace—"

"Bryce will get out of those silly auditions!" a woman's gruff voice cut in. "Trust me!"

The girls exchanged surprised looks. The familiar voice was coming from behind the plant.

Quietly, Nancy, Bess, and George spread the leaves apart. Sitting in a velvet chair, with her back to the plant, was Cookie. She pressed a silver cell phone to her ear as she spoke loudly. "If you want to deliver that movie script to our hotel suite, it's number three-one-eight."

Cookie clicked off her phone. She then accepted a cup of coffee that a hotel worker brought to her.

The girls let the leaves spring back.

"Forget about asking Cookie questions," George whispered. "Let's go up to room three-one-eight and look for clues."

"Her room will be locked for sure," Nancy whispered. "How will we get inside?"

"We'll figure it out," George whispered.

The girls rode the elevator up to the third floor. They ran down the carpeted hall until they found room 318.

A cart filled with towels and cleaning supplies stood in front of the door. The housekeeper was working on the room. And the door was open!

"Are we lucky or what?" George smiled.

The girls backed against the wall just as the housekeeper stepped out. As she collected fresh towels they slipped through the doorway and inside the room.

"The housekeeper is coming back," Nancy hissed.

The girls crouched behind a big, cushy chair. One by one they peeked out over the back. Sure enough, the housekeeper was in the room. But after hanging towels in the bathroom, she left and slammed the door shut.

Nancy, Bess, and George darted out from behind the chair. Bess opened a door to find another room.

"This must be Bryce's room," Bess pointed out.

"How do you know?" Nancy asked.

"It's messy—like all boys' rooms," Bess said.

"Hey!" George complained. "My room is messy, but I'm not a boy."

Nancy peeked inside the room. On top of Bryce's dresser were half a dozen bottles of Fruity Fizzy juice.

"He really does drink that stuff," Nancy said.

"You guys!" George called from Cookie's room. "Look what I found inside Cookie's trash can."

She was holding up a plastic bag—a bag from Yuks Joke Shop!

"Bingo!" Nancy declared. But her smile turned into a frown when they heard a click.

"The lock!" George looked panicked.

"Someone's coming!" Bess groaned.

The girls crouched behind the bed just as the door opened. In a flash the girls crawled underneath the bed. As soon as they did, though, Bess screamed.

"There's somebody under here!" Bess cried.

CHAPTER FIVE

Gloom Service

It was dark and dusty under the bed. But after blinking once or twice, Nancy could see their classmate Shelby Metcalf!

"What are you doing here?" Nancy whispered.

"I snuck in to wait for Bryce," Shelby whispered back. "Just like you did."

"We're not waiting for Bryce," George whispered, sliding under the bed toward Shelby. "We're— Owwwww!"

George yelped as she banged her head on the underside of the bed. All four girls froze until . . .

"Hey! Who's there?" Cookie's voice demanded.

"Busted," Shelby sighed.

Cookie planted her hands on her hips as the girls crawled out from under the bed. "You fans just can't keep away, can you?" she demanded.

"We're not fans!" Nancy said. "I mean, we are—but that's not why we're here."

"We're detectives," George said. She pointed her thumb at Shelby. "Except for this one."

"I'm just a fan," Shelby said with a smile. "Will Bryce be here soon? Can he sign my sneakers? Pleeeease?"

Nancy stepped in front of Shelby and said, "We want to find out who's ruining the *Kids Can Dance!* auditions."

"I don't know what you're talking about." Cookie stared hard at Nancy.

George lifted the plastic Yuks bag from the trash can. "Perhaps this will help ring a bell?" she asked.

"That's not mine!" Cookie insisted. "Why would I shop at a joke store?"

"Then what did you mean when you said Bryce won't be judging the *Kids Can Dance!* auditions?" Bess asked.

Cookie's eyebrows flew up.

"Were you listening in on my phone conversation?" Cookie demanded. She held up her cell phone. "Give me your telephone numbers. I'm calling your parents right now!"

The girls gave one another worried looks. Then Bess turned to Cookie and said sweetly, "We were just leaving." The girls shot out of the room. As they ran toward the elevator Nancy heard Cookie's door slam.

"All that trouble, and we didn't even find Bryce!" Shelby wailed as they filed into the elevator.

"But we did find that Yuks bag in Cookie's

room," Nancy whispered to Bess and George. "And that's a great clue!"

Nancy, Bess, and George said good-bye to Shelby. They left the hotel and made their way up River Street.

"How about some pizza?" George asked. "All that sneaking, hiding, and yelling made me hungry."

"Let's go the theater instead," Nancy said.

"The auditions aren't for another hour," Bess pointed out.

"Exactly!" Nancy said. "If the troublemaker strikes, he or she will probably strike before the auditions."

But as the girls headed toward the Spotlight Theater someone began walking toward them. It was Henderson carrying a big plastic bag with both hands.

"Another bag from Yuks," Nancy noted.

Nancy, Bess, and George raced toward Henderson. He stared at the girls as he shifted the bag in his hands.

"What's up?" Henderson asked.

"What's in the bag?" Nancy asked.

"It looks pretty heavy," Bess added.

"What if I don't want to show you what's in the bag?" Henderson asked coolly.

"What if we don't care?" George said, grabbing one side of the bag and pulling. Henderson grunted and held on to the other side.

Nancy and Bess watched the tug-of-war. George and Henderson dug their heels into the ground as they pulled.

"You were shopping at Yuks so you could ruin

the auditions!" George shouted at Henderson.

"You're crazy!" Henderson shouted out. His knuckles were white as he held on to his side of the bag.

"Nancy! Bess!" George shouted over her shoulder. "Why are you just standing there? Grab on!"

"Three against one wouldn't be fair," Bess said.

But as George began losing her grip on the bag, Nancy ran over. She grabbed George's waist and began to pull.

"Not me!" George shouted. "Grab the bag!"

The plastic bag ripped in half. Nancy and George flew back, knocking into Bess.

"Ooof!" Bess grunted as all three friends tumbled to the ground in a heap.

"Now look what you did!" Henderson said. "He'll never take it back if it's dirty!"

"Take what back?" Nancy asked as they stood up. She saw Henderson pointing to his ice-cream cone costume. It was lying on the sidewalk next to a pair of black shoes.

"I asked Mr. Decker if he'd take back my costume and shoes, and he said yes," Henderson wailed. "I was on my way to do it when you guys barged in!"

"Why are you bringing it back?" George asked. "Aren't you auditioning for *Kids Can Dance!* too?"

"Not anymore!" Henderson declared. "I quit!"

"Quit the auditions?" Nancy asked. "But your dad needed the prize money for that pretzel truck."

"No, he doesn't," Henderson said.

"Yes, he does!" Nancy, Bess, and George said together.

Just then Nancy heard the sound of jingling bells. It sounded like the Mr. Drippy truck getting closer and closer. But as the truck turned onto River Street, Nancy didn't see the usual spinning ice-cream cone on the roof. Instead she saw a giant spinning pretzel!

"Girls," Henderson said, puffing out his chest, "say hello to Mr. Twisty!"

CHaPTER Six

Oiled and Foiled

The truck stopped, and Mr. Murphy leaned out the window. "I've got thirty-two pretzel flavors—get them while they're hot!" he shouted.

"You didn't win the prize money yet, Henderson," George said. "How did your dad get the pretzel truck?"

"He won the River Heights lottery on Thursday," Henderson said proudly. "Who needs the prize money now?"

"That's why you quit the dance contest?" Nancy asked.

"You bet!" Henderson said. "I'm returning my dorky costume today if Mr. Decker takes it back."

While Henderson gathered up his costume, the girls compared notes.

"His story does add up," Nancy said. "Why would he be in the dance contest if he doesn't need the money anymore?"

George grabbed both shoes before Henderson could pick them up.

"The taps are still on," George said, turning

them over. "So Henderson couldn't have stuck them on Deirdre's ballet shoes."

Nancy agreed. Henderson hadn't ruined the dance auditions. And she hoped they hadn't ruined his costume.

"Sorry, Henderson," Nancy apologized. "But we have to find out who's ruining the *Kids Can Dance!* auditions."

"Well, nothing can ruin this great day," Henderson declared with a wide grin. "My dancing days are *over*."

Henderson gave his dad a wave before walking off toward Yuks.

"Step right up, girls!" Mr. Murphy shouted. "Mr. Twisty's are the only pretzels worth their salt."

Nancy stared at the list of pretzel flavors on the side of the truck. He really did have thirty-two flavors. But then she saw something else— pasted on the side of the truck was the winning lottery ticket. The date on it was Thursday, just like Henderson said.

The girls bought one pretzel each.

"I've never tasted a pistachio pretzel before," George said. "Next time I'm trying the rocky road."

When Nancy, Bess, and George reached the theater, Lou stood in front of the door. He shook his head when they asked to go inside.

"Mindy and the judges are having their pre-production meeting," Lou explained. "No one can bother them."

"But I left something in the pocket of my pink trench coat," Bess said.

"What?" Lou asked.

"Um . . . my gum?" Bess said.

"Gum's not important," Lou said.

"*Her* gum is!" George piped in. "It's a special vitamin gum she has to chew."

Nancy bit her lip to keep from giggling, but it worked. Lou stepped away from the door and said, "Go ahead. And make it snappy."

The girls rushed through the door into the theater. Nancy could see Mindy, Nigel, and Ivy sitting and talking in the back. But where was Bryce?

Nancy, Bess, and George slipped backstage where the dancers' costumes and props were kept. There was nobody else in the room.

Nancy glanced up at the shelves. One had stacks of music CDs including their own, labeled SECRET AGENT GIRLS.

"Look at what I found," Bess called. She held up a pair of ballet shoes. "They were in the garbage."

"Deirdre's ballet slippers," Nancy said, running over to Bess. "She probably threw them away after they were ruined with those taps."

Nancy took a ballet slipper from Bess. She flipped it over.

"A bottle cap," Nancy said, wrinkling

her nose because she had expected to find steel taps.

Bess turned the other slipper over and said, "This shoe has a bottle cap glued on too."

Nancy read the bottle cap out loud. "Fruity Fizzy . . . that's the stuff that Bryce drinks."

"How do you know?" a boy's voice asked.

The girls whirled around. "Bryce!" they said at the same time.

He stood in front of them wearing his *Middle School Meltdown* jacket. "How're you doing?" he asked.

"F-f-fine!" Bess stammered.

"Wh-wh-wh-what are you doing here?" Nancy asked.

"Looking for a snack," Bryce said. "But there's nothing back here."

"Um—there's a pretzel truck outside," Bess squeaked. "D-d-do you like pretzels?"

George rolled her eyes at Nancy and Bess as if to say, *Stop asking dumb questions.*

"Do you dance at your real school like you

dance on *Middle School Meltdown?"* George asked Bryce.

"I wish I could go to a real school," Bryce sighed. "I have a tutor instead. My mom."

"Your mom?" Nancy asked, surprised.

"No wonder you want to go to a real school," George mumbled under her breath.

"Gotta run," Bryce said. He gave a little wave and left the room. After a few seconds Nancy and Bess began jumping up and down.

"He spoke to us! Bryce Brown spoke to us!" Nancy cried.

"Will you forget about Bryce?" George groaned. "We have to look for clues before Lou comes searching for us." She stepped forward and then shouted, "Whooooaaaaa!"

Nancy turned to see George slipping over a small puddle on the floor.

"Are you okay?" Nancy asked.

"Yeah," George said, standing up. "I just stepped on something slippery."

"Here's probably why," Nancy said. She

picked up an uncapped travel-size bottle of baby oil from a high shelf not far from the puddle.

"What's that stuff doing backstage?" George asked.

Nancy didn't think the bottle of oil was a big deal. But just as she put it back, she heard a rustling noise.

Turning toward the noise she saw Gina Gleason's huge hoop skirt. It was hanging from a hook on the wall.

Nancy's eyes traveled down until she saw a pair of grubby sneakers sticking out from underneath.

"Someone's under that skirt," Nancy whispered.

The Clue Crew inched over to the hoop skirt. Nancy reached down and lifted the ruffled hem.

"Phoebe!" Nancy exclaimed.

Their suspect looked scared as she jumped to her feet.

"Don't tell anyone I was hiding here," Phoebe begged the girls. "Pleeeeease!"

CHAPTER SEVEN

Phoebe's Heebie-Jeebies

"We know why you're hiding, Phoebe," George said. "So you could ruin the dancers' costumes and props."

"No way!" Phoebe exclaimed.

Nancy looked down at Phoebe. She'd never noticed how short she was until now.

"Then why were you hiding?" Nancy asked.

"So the dancers couldn't boss me around!" Phoebe cried. "You wouldn't believe what they make me do."

"Like what?" Bess asked.

"One dancer was wearing gloves, so she made me hold a tissue while she blew her nose!" Phoebe exclaimed.

"Ew," Bess said. "Sorry I asked."

Nancy had one other question to ask Phoebe. "Were you hiding back here all alone?"

"At first I was," Phoebe replied, "until someone came back here. I couldn't see who it was, but I heard whistling like this. . . ."

Phoebe puckered her lips and whistled a tune.

"I've never heard it before," Nancy admitted.

"Me neither," George said. "But it has a good beat."

The door swung open and a bunch of kids stormed into the room.

"Hey, Phoebe," a fifth-grade girl called. "We're auditioning today, so you'd better be on your toes."

"Here we go again," Phoebe groaned.

"Yo, Phoebe," Antonio chuckled. "Hold this for us, will you?"

Antonio shoved a rubber tarantula into Phoebe's palm. Phoebe shrieked as she flung it to the side.

"I don't think Phoebe ruined the auditions," Nancy whispered. "She'd have to be a lot taller to reach the really high shelves."

Phoebe was already handing out water bottles when Mindy came backstage.

"Those of you not auditioning today please take your seats in the theater," Mindy announced.

"That means us," George said, starting to leave.

"Wait," Nancy told her friends. "Let's take our things so nothing happens to them."

The girls pulled their coats off the hangers, grabbed their magnifying glasses and music CD from the shelves, and carried them into the theater.

They were about to sit down when Nancy saw Cookie.

She was sitting in the back of the theater putting on lipstick.

"There's one of our suspects," Nancy pointed out.

"Watch out, Cookie," George muttered. "The Clue Crew will make you crumble."

Bryce, Nigel, and Ivy took their places at the judges' table. After a welcome from Mindy the auditions began.

French cancan music filled the theater as Kendra hurried onstage, dressed in her frilly blouse and skirt.

"Why is she walking so funny?" Nancy whispered.

"You'd walk funny too in those tight pointy boots," George whispered back.

Nancy didn't think it was the boots. Kendra looked more worried than in pain.

Ivy was clapping her hands to the music as Kendra waved her skirt back and forth.

Kendra lifted her right leg and gave a big kick. Her shoe went flying off her foot. It whizzed through the air until hitting— *whack*—Nigel's forehead!

"Cheese and crackers!" Nigel cried.

"It was an accident, really!" Kendra blurted. "My shoes were slippery inside. I don't know how it happened."

"Did Kendra just say 'slippery'?" Nancy whispered. "Slippery as in . . . oil?"

ChAPTER EighT

Hip-Hop Flop

"The bottle of baby oil we found backstage," Bess gasped as she remembered. "Maybe someone poured oil into Kendra's shoes when no one was around."

Nigel was still rubbing his head as Kendra ran offstage.

"Now my head hurts on the inside *and* the outside," Nigel groaned. "What's wrong with this town, anyway?"

Cookie marched down the aisle straight to Mindy. "Mindy, I demand you cancel the auditions in River Heights before more poor judges get hurt!" she declared.

"Mo-om," Bryce protested.

"Nice try, Cookie," Mindy said. "But the auditions are still on—no matter how bad these kids dance."

Nancy couldn't believe her ears! How rude!

"Mayor Strong?" Ivy called with a sweet smile. "Let's bring out the next act, shall we?"

"And get it over with!" Nigel snapped.

Mayor Strong cleared his throat before saying, "Yes . . . yes, of course. The next act will be Antonio Elefano and Peter Patino—the Rip-It-Up Robots!"

Antonio's and Peter's jumbo tin cans clattered as they ran onstage. Peter carried a boom box, which he placed on the floor. Antonio popped in a CD before pressing a button.

"The Rip-It-Up Robots are going to rock the house!" Peter shouted out to the audience.

"That's right—we're bad!" Antonio shouted too.

"They're bad, all right," Bess muttered.

The boys stood center stage, ready to pop and lock. Music blared from the boom box.

It wasn't a hip-hop beat, but a slow classical waltz!

"You grabbed the wrong CD, dweeb!" Antonio cried.

"Our names were on it!" Peter protested. "What are we going to do now?"

Antonio began waltzing to the music with an imaginary partner. Peter did the same as the audience howled with laughter. When the music stopped, the boys stopped waltzing to face the judges.

"Well," Ivy said. "That wasn't what I expected."

"Why am I not surprised?" Nigel huffed.

"I thought it was kind of funny," Bryce chuckled.

"What's so funny about someone switching our music?" Antonio asked with a scowl.

"Another excuse," Nigel scoffed. "Can we *switch* to the next act, please, Mindy?"

Peter grabbed the boom box. Both boys muttered under their breaths as they walked offstage.

"If someone ruined the boys' audition," Bess murmured, "Antonio and Peter probably didn't ruin the others."

"Then who's doing this?" George wondered.

Nancy looked around the theater for Cookie. But the mom-ager was nowhere to be seen.

"Let's go outside," Nancy whispered.

Carrying their gear, the girls slipped out of the theater before the next act. The first thing

Nancy saw was a long black limo parked at the curb. A sign underneath the windshield read: COOKIE BROWN.

"Cookie's car!" Bess pointed out.

The driver was leaning against the car eating a Mr. Twisty pretzel.

"Mmm, cherry vanilla!" the driver said to himself. When he saw the girls running over, he frowned. "Bryce is not in this car, so don't even think of ripping out the car seats trying to find him."

"We're not looking for Bryce," Nancy said. "We're looking for his mom. Did you see her?"

"Are you kidding?" the driver guffawed. "I drove her here twenty minutes ago."

"*Exactly* twenty minutes ago?" Nancy asked.

The driver put the pretzel on the hood of the car. He pulled out a little red book and flipped it open.

"See?" the driver asked. "I write down each arrival time so my passengers can't complain they were late."

Nancy studied the page. Cookie's name and the time were written neatly. She looked at her watch and did the math. Cookie did arrive twenty minutes ago. Exactly.

"Now can I go back to my pretzel?" the driver asked.

The girls thanked the driver, then stepped away from the car.

"Why was it so important what time Cookie got here, Nancy?" Bess asked.

"Because twenty minutes wasn't enough time for Cookie to go backstage and make trouble," Nancy explained. "Especially with the others backstage getting ready."

"Cookie was in the hotel before that," George pointed out. "We saw her there ourselves."

Nancy thought about Cookie as a suspect as the girls walked away from the theater. The timeline may not have added up, but other things did.

"There's still the Yuks bag we found in Cookie's room," Nancy said. "And we heard her say that Bryce would do the movie instead of the *Kids Can Dance!* auditions."

"So Cookie is still a suspect," George agreed.

Since all three girls had family plans that evening, Nancy suggested they work on the case first thing in the morning.

"Are you forgetting what tomorrow is?" Bess asked.

"Sunday," George said with a shrug.

"It's the day we're auditioning," Bess reminded them. "We have to practice tomorrow morning whether the case is solved or not."

Nancy knew Bess was right. They had spent so much time on the case they'd forgotten to practice!

"Okay," Nancy said with a smile. "We'll practice first thing tomorrow morning."

The three friends waited for Hannah to pick them up. Nancy still wanted to work on the case the next day. But she also wanted to make it through the *Kids Can Dance!* auditions.

"What kind of pizza should we order, Daddy?" Nancy asked Saturday evening. "Pepperoni, mushroom, or veggie?"

"Whatever you want, Nancy!" Mr. Drew said as he drove the car. "This is your good-luck dinner for the audition tomorrow."

"We'll need all the luck we can get," Nancy sighed.

"Why?" Mr. Drew asked, turning the steering wheel. "You are practicing tomorrow, aren't you?"

"I'd rather work on our case, Daddy," Nancy admitted. "What if the troublemaker strikes tomorrow? What if he or she pours mushy oatmeal in the pockets of our pink coats?"

"No worries," Mr. Drew chuckled. "Sometimes clues pop up when you're not even looking."

"Well, they'd better pop up fast, Daddy," Nancy said as she turned on the radio. It was set to her favorite station, RIV-FM.

Instead of a song, she heard the DJ's speedy voice say, "The wait is over to hear Bryce

Brown's new song from his new CD. It's the first time we're playing it, and the first time you're hearing it!"

"Cool!" Nancy said with a smile.

Bryce's singing voice filled the car. Nancy was sure she had heard the tune before. But how could she if this was the first time the radio was playing it?

Suddenly it clicked!

I know! Nancy thought excitedly. *This is the song Phoebe heard someone whistling backstage!*

Was it Bryce whistling his new song?

He's tall enough to reach the shelves, Nancy thought, her eyes widening. *And he's in the theater every day!*

"Omigosh!" Nancy gasped quietly. "Could the person making all the trouble be Bryce Brown?"

ChAPTER NiNE

Jacket Racket

"Did you just say something, Nancy?" Mr. Drew asked as he drove the car. "I thought I heard you say something about Bryce."

Nancy turned to her dad. She didn't want him to know what she was thinking.

"It was nothing, Daddy," Nancy blurted with a smile. "I was just singing along to Bryce's new song."

Mr. Drew parked the car right in front of Pizza Paradise. But a pepperoni and extra-cheese pizza was the furthest thing from Nancy's mind.

Bryce couldn't have done something so mean. He's too cool, Nancy thought as she unbuckled her seat belt. *What was I thinking?*

"Wrong, wrong, wrong!" Bess said as she pressed the pause button on the boom box. "We're supposed to spin all the way around at the words 'secret agent girls.'"

"I thought that was the part when we wave our magnifying glasses," George said.

"I thought that was the part when we hop three times," Nancy said.

It was early Sunday morning, but the girls had already been practicing for forty-five minutes in George's room. Their big audition was just a few hours away.

"And why do we have to wear the pink coats?" George asked. "It's only a rehearsal."

"A *dress* rehearsal," Bess declared.

Nancy and George took their places as Bess restarted the music.

"Where's my magnifying glass?" Bess asked. She pointed to George's bed, still unmade. "I put it right there before I turned off the music."

A loud flushing noise suddenly came from George's bathroom.

"Who's in there?" George called.

All three girls peeked into the bathroom.

"Ew," Nancy said.

George's baby brother was trying to flush Bess's magnifying glass down the toilet.

"Scott!" Bess shouted. "What are you doing?"

Two-year-old Scott pointed to the magnifying glass in the toilet. "It floats like my toy boat!" he said happily.

George shrugged and said, "He's being toilet trained."

"Well, it's not working," Bess cried.

"Mommy!!!" Scott cried. Wailing, he ran out of the bathroom and George's bedroom.

"Just dry it off, Bess," George said. She was about to reach into the toilet when Bess grabbed her arm.

"Ew, George! No way will I use that icky, germy spyglass," Bess said. "I want a brand-new *clean* one."

Nancy couldn't blame Bess. So on the way to the audition, the girls stopped at Yuks Joke Shop.

"It's your lucky day, girls," Mr. Decker said, this time wearing fake glasses with springy eyeballs. "I've got one more giant magnifying glass in the back room."

Bryce's picture still hung on the wall behind the counter. While Mr. Decker went to the back room, the girls slipped behind the counter for a better look.

"What did Cookie write on this one?" Nancy asked.

Bess's eyes widened as she studied the writing on the picture. "Cookie didn't write this one," she said.

"What do you mean?" Nancy asked.

"The handwriting on that picture is really Bryce's," Bess insisted.

"So Bryce was in Yuks Joke Shop?" George asked.

Nancy remembered her thoughts about Bryce last night. It was time to share them with the Clue Crew.

"You guys!" Nancy blurted. "The song Phoebe heard someone whistling was Bryce's new song—one that nobody had heard before. And Bryce is tall enough to reach those shelves, and the bottle caps on Deirdre's ballet slippers were Fruity Fizzy—the juice Bryce drinks."

"Wait a minute, wait a minute," George said.

"Are you saying the person who ruined the auditions is Bryce?"

"Yuks is only a few blocks away from the Glitz-Morton Hotel," Nancy pointed out.

"How would Bryce sneak all that stuff into the theater?" Bess asked. "The rubber roaches, the itching powder—"

"Pockets!" George cut in. "That's why he wore that *Middle School Meltdown* jacket to the auditions every day."

"And while the other judges were having their meetings," Nancy went on, "Bryce snuck backstage to make trouble."

Bess stared at Bryce's picture sadly. "Not Bryce!" she wailed. "He's too cute to ruin the auditions—"

"If we don't stop Bryce, he'll ruin our audition," Nancy cut in. "Come on, let's go!"

The girls raced for the door just as Mr. Decker came out from the back room.

"What about the magnifying glass?" Mr. Decker shouted as they bolted from the store.

❀ ❀ ❀

When Nancy, Bess, and George reached the theater, they were not alone. Crowded outside were kids—mostly girls.

"What's going on?" Nancy asked.

The girls pushed through the crowd. Standing in front of the theater were Mayor Strong, Mindy, Cookie, and Bryce.

Cookie pulled a *Middle School Meltdown* jacket from a cardboard box and shouted, "Come on, kids! Whoever knows the most about Bryce wins a jacket signed by me—I mean, Bryce!"

Bryce stood near his mom, his hands dug into the pockets of his own jacket.

"Look at how stuffed Bryce's pockets are," Nancy said above the adoring screams. "If only we could get our hands on his jacket."

Bryce stepped forward and smiled. "Okay, first trivia question!" he called out. "When is my birthday?"

Hands shot up, including Bess's. But their

friend Marcy Rubin yelled from the crowd, "It's September eighth!"

"Correct!" Bryce said, pointing to Marcy.

"Awwwwww," the crowd groaned as Marcy ran to get her jacket. She waved it in the air before Cookie gave her a little push to move on.

"Don't worry, you guys, the fun has just begun!" Bryce called out. "Next question—what's my middle name?"

"Williaaaaaaaam!!!" Bess screamed so loud that Nancy and George had to cover their ears.

"The little lady aced the test!" Bryce said, smiling at Bess. "Come up and get your jacket!"

Nancy smiled as Bess pushed her way over to Bryce.

"Here," Cookie said, holding out a jacket.

"Nuh-uh!" Bess said, shaking her head. She pointed to Bryce. "I want *that* jacket!"

Nancy and George traded excited looks. Bess had the correct answer—and a plan!

"But . . . this is my jacket," Bryce said, digging his hands deeper into his pockets.

"That's why I want it!" Bess said with a grin.

"Give it to her, Bryce," Cookie said. "It'll be great for publicity."

"And we have a news reporter here," Mayor Strong said. He snapped his fingers at a photographer, who quickly snapped a shot.

"I'd rather not give her my jacket," Bryce said, shaking his head. "It's got a jelly-donut stain on it—"

"A stain Bryce Brown made!" Bess shrieked. "Even better!"

"You got it, honey," Cookie said. She marched over to Bryce and started to tug the jacket off his shoulders.

"Mo-om!" Bryce whined.

Cookie grunted as she struggled with the jacket. She gave one last tug and stuff began spilling out of Bryce's pockets onto the ground.

Nancy, Bess, and George stared at the sidewalk and gasped. There were squirting carnations, a plastic snake, a bar of trick green soap, and much, much more.

"Where did that come from?" Cookie asked.

"All that stuff," Nancy declared, "is from Yuks!"

"Yuks?" Cookie cried.

"It's joke stuff," Nancy explained. "That bag from Yuks wasn't yours. It was Bryce's."

Bryce heaved a big sigh and said, "Oh boy."

ChAPTER TEN

Let's Dance!

"We think Bryce ruined the *Kids Can Dance!* auditions," George said.

"That is ridiculous!" Cookie scoffed.

"Girls," the mayor said with a nervous laugh, "why don't you all take a jacket and run along?"

"We just want the truth," Bess said.

"Bryce?" Mindy asked. "Did you sabotage the auditions?"

Bryce hesitated. "Kind of."

Everyone gasped, including Cookie. Mindy stepped forward and said, "Why, Bryce?"

"I didn't want to go from town to town the next few weeks judging the *Kids Can Dance!* auditions!" Bryce said.

"I knew it!" Cookie laughed. "Bryce wants to do the blockbuster movie in Hollywood instead, right, sweetie?"

"No way, Mom!" Bryce said, shaking his head. "I want to go back to school this fall with my friends. Like I used to before I became a star."

That's when Nancy remembered what he'd told them backstage.

"Bryce is telling the truth, Mayor," Nancy said. "He really does want to go back to school."

"For sure," Bess said with a smile. "He wants a real teacher, not a tutor like—"

George interrupted Bess with an elbow jab. But Cookie's eyebrows had already flown up.

"A tutor like me?" Cookie demanded. "What's wrong with my tutoring, Bryce? Who taught you how to use a BlackBerry?"

"It's not the same, Mom," Bryce insisted. "I want to learn math and social studies, and go to gym class. I even want to take pop quizzes."

"Pop quizzes?" George said, wrinkling her nose. "Wow. He really *does* want to go to school."

"But what about *Middle School Meltdown*?" Cookie asked, shaking her son's arm. "You're the star of the show."

"*Meltdown* films during summer vacation so the kids in the show *can* go to school," Bryce explained. "All the other stuff like recording sessions and interviews I can do *after* school."

"Sounds like a plan!" Mayor Strong boomed. "What do you say, Cookie?"

Nancy held her breath as they waited for Cookie's answer. Finally the mom-ager shrugged and said, "It won't hurt to say yes."

Nancy, Bess, and George cheered along with Bryce's fans. But no one looked happier than Bryce himself. "Thanks, Mom!" Bryce exclaimed.

"It's okay with me, too," Mindy said with a nod. "Bryce can break his contract if he'd like."

"I'll finish the auditions here in River Heights first," Bryce promised. "It's only fair."

"Fair?" a girl's voice shouted. The voice came from Kendra, pushing her way through the crowd. "Bryce ruined our auditions!" Kendra shouted. "What's so fair about that?"

"How would he like to itch like a dog with fleas?" a fifth-grade cheerleader shouted.

"Or look like a jerk in front of all your friends?" Peter yelled.

Bryce's face burned red. "I'm sorry, guys," he sighed. "Anything I can do to make it up . . ."

An idea popped into Nancy's head. "There is, Bryce," Nancy piped up. "I know a way you can make it up and go to school at the same time."

"How?" Bryce asked.

"You can sing at school assembly tomorrow morning," Nancy said.

Excited whispers filled the air.

"That would be awesome," Bryce said, turning to his mother. "Is that okay with you, Mom?"

"It would be great publicity!" Cookie replied. Her face softened as she added, "Or just fun."

"Yes!" Nancy cheered under her breath.

Mayor Strong put his arm around Bryce's shoulders and said, "I'm sure you'll get a very warm welcome!" The girls traded high fives.

Nancy turned to Mindy and said, "Bring on the auditions!" Lou flung the theater door open, and the kids filed in. The girls were already in their costumes, so they auditioned first.

As their song, "Secret Agent Girls," played, the girls danced for the judges. Bess didn't mind not having a magnifying glass. It gave her a chance to snap her fingers to the beat.

After everyone auditioned, the judges made their final decisions.

"And the winners are," Bryce announced, "the fifth-grade cheerleaders."

"We could tell what good dancers they really were," Ivy said. "Even with the itching powder."

"And good dancers don't come easy in River Heights," Nigel added, winking at the audience as if to say, "Kidding!"

Nancy, Bess, and George were sad they didn't win but happy about many other things. The Clue Crew had solved another case and helped Bryce get his wish. They'd even gotten to see how talented their friends and schoolmates were.

"Who knew our friends could burn the floor like that?" George asked as the Clue Crew left the Spotlight Theater.

"I guess kids *can* dance!" Bess said.

"Yeah!" Nancy agreed with a smile. "And they definitely can solve mysteries."

TAP, TAP, HOORAY!

So you think you can dance? Before you shuffle off to Buffalo, check out these cool tap shoes you can make yourself!

You will need:

Old pair of shoes that fit snugly on your feet. (No flip-flops or bunny slippers!)

Four juice bottle caps or small jar lids. (The almost-flat kind without any sharp edges.)

Adhesive putty or craft glue. (Make sure you no longer need the shoe before you glue!)

Let's get dancing!

❀ Turn shoes upside down, soles up.

❀ Using putty or glue, stick a bottle cap near the toe and heel parts of your shoes.

❀ Wait until glue dries. (Use this time to pick out some tap-happy music or research some tap-dance steps.)

❀ Put on your new tap shoes and some music—then dance like no one's watching!

Tips for tap: Want to really jazz up your new tap shoes? Decorate them with gold or silver glitter. Or add a shiny shoelace for that touch of Broadway glitz!